Move Over, Wheelchairs Coming Through!

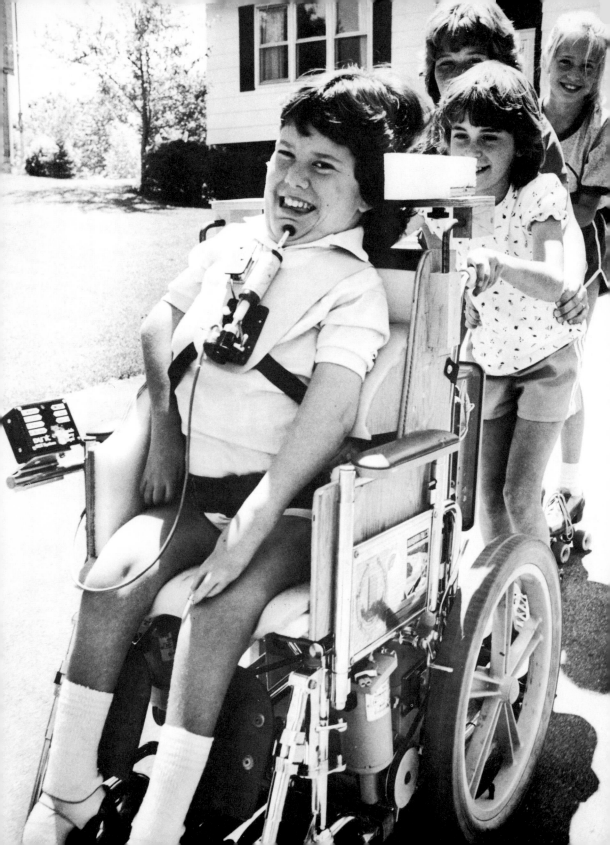

Move Over, Wheelchairs Coming Through!

Seven Young People in Wheelchairs
Talk About Their Lives

BY RON ROY

Photographs by Rosmarie Hausherr

Clarion Books

TICKNOR & FIELDS: A HOUGHTON MIFFLIN COMPANY

New York

Clarion Books
Ticknor & Fields, a Houghton Mifflin Company

Library of Congress Cataloging in Publication Data
Roy, Ron, 1940–
    Move over, wheelchairs coming through!

    Summary: Text and photographs present seven disabled youngsters between the ages
of nine and nineteen who use wheelchairs in their fully active lives at home, at school,
and on vacation.
    1. Physically handicapped children—Juvenile literature. [1. Physically handi-
capped. 2. Wheelchairs] I. Hausherr, Rosmarie, ill. II. Title
HV903.R69 1985   362.4′3′088054   84-14314
ISBN 0-89919-249-1

Q 10 9 8 7 6 5 4 3 2

Thank you, Elizabeth, Jeff, Tammy, Liz, Scott, Mark and José. This book is for you.

—R.R. and R.H.

Author's Note

While writing this book, I talked with dozens of people who willingly offered their help: nurses, doctors, therapists, teachers, parents, psychologists, hospital aides and administrators. Everyone I asked gave valuable assistance, without which this book could not have been written. Many thanks to these people for their advice, patience, time and concern for people with disabilities.

But it is to the seven young people profiled in this book that I owe the most gratitude. During the many hours I spent talking with them and their families, I was made to feel welcome in their homes. Even when my questions became personal, I was given honest, candid answers.

Contents

Kids and Wheelchairs

*T*housands of kids are wheelchair users. These young people are disabled, but in most cases their disabilities have not stopped them from doing the things they want to do. If a wheelchair can get there, wheelchair *users* can get there.

And they do. They swim, play basketball or other sports, travel across the city or country. Many disabled kids accompany their able-bodied friends to movies, concerts, ball games, museums, or the beach. Some even drive there in their own cars.

A number of wheelchair users get around by using their hands to wheel their chairs. Others use battery-powered wheelchairs operated with a control lever positioned on the chair arm. One girl in this book has a computerized wheelchair. She activates the computer by pressing a button with her chin. Many wheelchair users rely on friends and family to push their chairs for them.

But the fact is, wheelchair users of all ages do get around.

There are, however, many obstacles that make life tough for wheelchair users. These include narrow doorways, buildings without ramps or elevators, high thresholds, roadside curbs, drawers and shelves that are too high or too low, and buses unequipped to pick up wheelchair passengers.

In 1973 and 1975, two laws were passed by the United States federal government that help all disabled people, including the seven young people in this book. Section 504 of the Rehabilitation Act of 1973 prohibits any organizations that receive federal money (this includes schools) from discriminating in any way against persons with disabilities. An important part of Section 504 has to do with "architectural accessibility." This means that public buildings, including schools, must provide ramps or elevators so that mobility-impaired people are able to enter, move about the building, and leave.

The Federal Education For All Handicapped Children Act of 1975 provides for many guarantees and safeguards of the educational rights of disabled children. This act, referred to as Public Law 94–142, states that all handicapped children must receive a free public education. This education will be provided under the least confining and most normalized circumstances. That means that whenever possible for the good of the child, he or she should be mainstreamed into regular classes.

Able-bodied people sometimes want to help wheelchair users and other disabled people. It's usually easier for an able-bodied person to reach a high shelf for a can of beans.

Or carry an armload of books down a hallway crowded with school kids.

But some people who want to help someone using a wheelchair feel embarrassed. They can't think of what to say, or they may be afraid of being rejected. Others are simply afraid to approach a disabled person. They don't have a logical reason, usually. But when they see someone in a wheelchair they may cross the street, slip into a store, or walk in the other direction.

Striking up a conversation with a disabled person *can* feel awkward. How do you begin? What do you talk about? If the other person is in a wheelchair, should you sit down, too? Is it all right to ask about his or her disability?

The kids in this book are glad to talk about themselves. And they prefer to have someone ask them about their disability instead of staring at them. But they'd rather discuss other things. Like sports, TV shows and the latest movies, food, and making friends. The seven wheelchair users in this book all feel the same way: "Think of me as a person, not just as a disabled person. I'm interested in some of the same things you are. Talk to me."

The next time you see a person with a disability, why not talk to him or her? You may find an avid sports fan or a dedicated moviegoer, but best of all, you just might find a new friend.

Elizabeth Kaser

*I*t was snowing in Marcellus Knolls, New York. Lizzy, who was eight years old at the time, watched the snow from her wheelchair in the family room. She wanted to play in the snow, but she knew her wheelchair's computer and motor would be ruined if they got wet.

Then Lizzy's twelve-year-old brother, Josef, carried a large pan of snow into the kitchen. Now she could play in the snow — until it melted! Josef made two forts and tiny snowballs. He and Lizzy had a make-believe miniature snow fight, using Ken and Barbie dolls. Lizzy moved her play people about with her mouth and teeth, because she cannot move her fingers, hands or arms.

Lizzy and Josef have outgrown this snow game, but Lizzy, now ten, still uses her mouth and teeth for many activities. She was born with a condition called *arthrogryposis*. Lizzy can speak and move all parts of her head. But she cannot use her hands or arms, feet or legs. She gets around in a wheelchair operated by a computer attached to the back.

When Lizzy moves her chin downward, she can press a switch to activate the computer and motor. This is how Lizzy goes from room to room in her house, and from classroom to classroom in her school.

Lizzy uses her expensive wheelchair mostly at school or when she's outdoors in good weather. In the house, she prefers to lie on the floor or sit up in a chair.

Lizzy's family had a small elevator installed, outside the kitchen door of their home, to lift Lizzy and her wheelchair up to the entrance. This is how she leaves the house for

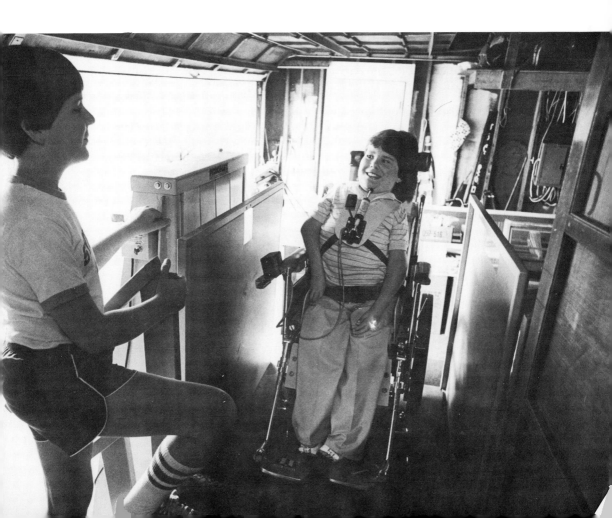

school in the morning and how she enters again in the afternoon. Lizzy can't use the elevator without help. Someone has to activate the elevator itself and hold the kitchen door open. Since there are no ramps leading up to the doors on the house, this elevator is Lizzy's only way to get in and out.

Inside the house, Lizzy depends on her parents and her brother for help. But she does a lot of things by herself. She uses her teeth and lips the way other kids use their fingers.

When she was about three years old, Lizzy began playing with toys and dolls by moving them about with her mouth. Her mother sewed Velcro fastenings into her dolls' clothing, so Lizzy could dress the dolls using her teeth. She soon became an expert at changing their outfits.

Lizzy learned to color by clamping her teeth down on a plastic cigarette holder with a crayon sticking out the other end. She does her homework while lying on the floor with a long pencil in her mouth. She has learned to type by punching the typewriter keys with a dowel held in her teeth. She can turn book pages, using the same dowel with an eraser attached to the end.

When Lizzy and Josef play board games, she picks up the pieces and moves them around the board with her lips or teeth. Card games were more difficult for Lizzy until her father made her a card holder. Now Lizzy can pick up and replace each card separately. If Lizzy is working on a project that needs to be propped up, she sits in front of an easel.

On hot summer days, Lizzy likes to cool off in a neighbor's pool. With one of her parents there to support her body, she likes to float on her back. Sometimes her mother helps her sit on the edge of the pool, then plop in. As long as an adult is with her, she is not afraid.

Lizzy tells her friends to splash her, dive over her, play water monster, and grab her toes underwater. "It makes me feel like I'm really swimming," Lizzy says. "The water feels good."

Lizzy is usually surrounded by her family or friends who help her, but one day her parents went shopping and left her at home. Josef was off playing with his friends, and Lizzy was in the garage in her wheelchair with the garage door open.

Her orders were to stay put in the garage, but the temptation to do something entirely by herself was too great to resist.

Lizzy lowered her chin and activated her wheelchair. Now she was in front of the garage, still moving. Suddenly the wheelchair went rolling down the driveway toward the street. The chair has no brakes, and Lizzy couldn't use her arms to stop the wheels. The chair shot across the street and landed in a ditch on the other side.

She got a couple of bad bruises, but her wheelchair strap prevented her from falling out. Luckily, no cars were passing her driveway when her chair hurtled into the street.

Lizzy doesn't like to talk about this accident. She knows she has to show more caution. With her chin, Lizzy can set off an alarm on her chair when she is in trouble, but the noise can only be heard from a short distance.

Lizzy has a group of friends who visit her almost every day. If it's not raining outside or too cold, she goes to their houses also. One of her friends has a playhouse in her backyard. She and Lizzy have decorated the house, and often play in it. The door is wide enough to accommodate Lizzy's wheelchair or stroller, so this is a favorite getaway place.

Lizzy's friends often walk to the mall or the movies, and Lizzy goes with them. Sometimes they roller-skate, and Lizzy zooms along behind or in front of them in her wheelchair.

One autumn day, the girls decided to roll in the leaves.

Lizzy wanted to play too, so they covered her from head to toe with leaves, wheelchair and all. Lizzy loved it, but her mother got the job of vacuuming the crushed leaves out of Lizzy's chair seat and clothing.

The middle school that Lizzy goes to has two floors and no elevator. She is mainstreamed, which means she goes to regular classes with all the other kids in her grade. But she can't get to the library or home economics room in her wheelchair, because they are located on the second floor. Although she has a school aide who helps her with books, Lizzy is too heavy to carry up the stairs.

Right now Lizzy doesn't mind being inconvenienced about the library. But her parents feel that as she gets older she will grow frustrated. More and more she will find that her disability prevents her from going where she wants to go. For now, her school is trying various plans to see that Lizzy can do library and home economics work. One idea is to videotape classes that Lizzy can't attend. Another plan is to rotate classrooms, so that at times the library and home economics skills are being taught on the first floor.

Now that Lizzy is in the fifth grade, the games in gym class are livelier. It is not always safe for her to participate. Also, the outside gym area is not wheelchair accessible. Lizzy feels frustrated, because she enjoys gym class.

But the school is planning a new program in which Lizzy will be able to take part. Seven or eight children will be involved, and half of them will be wheelchair users. In some cases, special adaptations will be used on the wheelchairs, so the kids will be able to enjoy more gym class activities. Lizzy

is eager for this to happen. "I don't like being left out," she says. "Especially of things I enjoy."

Lizzy is a Girl Scout. The building where her troop meets is totally accessible to her wheelchair. She is the only disabled girl in her group, but she participates in all activities, even camp-outs. Lizzy's mother goes along on these outings, to help with Lizzy's dressing and use of the bathroom. But Lizzy sleeps with her friends in one room while her mother stays with the adults in another.

Lizzy's parents are investigating new devices for her wheelchair. One possibility is a telephone. The phone would be hooked into the computer, and Lizzy would operate it with her chin. She would be able to make and receive calls, in the house or outside. "I can't wait," Lizzy says. "Now I have to ask someone to dial for me, and I have no privacy."

A slightly more complicated device would allow Lizzy to operate the house lights, television set, even the elevator outside the kitchen door. This equipment is very expensive, but Lizzy's parents are willing to make the financial investment to assure more independence for Lizzy as she grows older.

But Lizzy says she doesn't think too much about her future. She tries to enjoy herself every day. "I'm too young to think about jobs or college or getting married," Lizzy says. "I'm only ten!"

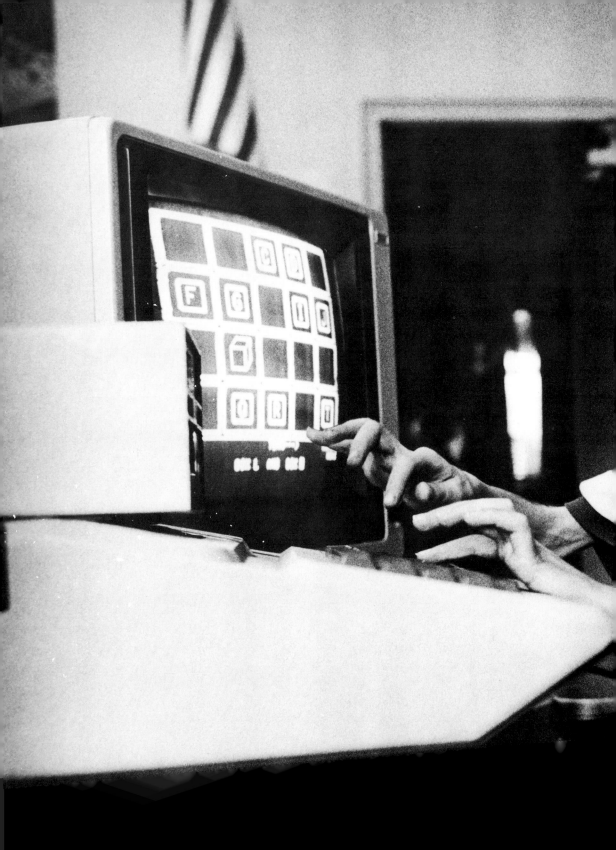

Jeff VanDusen

Jeff VanDusen loves country-western music. His favorite
singer is Kenny Rogers. When Kenny came to perform in the
Carrier Dome in Syracuse, New York, Jeff's family attended
the performance. So did thousands of other people; the dome
was packed with over 30,000 country-music lovers.

Because Jeff cannot walk, he uses a wheelchair. His parents telephoned the dome ahead of time to make sure there
were ramps and elevators. They were told that the dome was
wheelchair accessible. But when Jeff and his family arrived,
they realized that finding the elevators with thousands of
people milling around would not be easy. Also, they were
afraid that someone might accidentally bump Jeff's legs if he
were sitting in his wheelchair. They decided to leave the
wheelchair in the car and to carry Jeff to his seat. Jeff had to
depend on his parents for everything that evening, even
when he needed to use the boys' bathroom.

"Being carried was okay with me," Jeff said. "It was scary with all those people walking around. I'm glad I got to hear Kenny sing."

Jeff has had a struggle since the day he was born. His hips and knees are dislocated. He has a condition called *hemolymphangioma*, which causes large bumps on his body. For the first year and a half of his life, Jeff had weights attached to his legs so his hips and knees would line up properly.

Now Jeff is eight, and the struggle is not over. He has had over forty-five operations since he was born. About twenty-five of these operations were on Jeff's knees and hips. The rest were for removing some of the tumors on his body.

Even though Jeff was able to walk from age two to age four, he now uses a wheelchair all the time. His legs are too weak to hold him up, because of all the operations he has had on his hips and knees. Each time Jeff had surgery, he had to stay in bed for a long time. While he was in bed, his leg muscles grew weaker.

Jeff lives with his mother and father and two brothers, Dan and Jamie. Their house is surrounded by a big lawn and thick woods. Jeff's wheelchair can't follow his brothers as they explore the woods, but with their help he can play in the yard.

Jeff likes baseball, but a regular bat is too heavy for him so he uses a plastic one. One of his brothers pitches. When Jeff gets a hit, his other brother runs the bases. They use a plastic whiffle ball or a tennis ball in case a wild pitch hits Jeff instead of his bat.

When Dan and Jamie are off by themselves, Jeff plays

alone. His school friends don't live close enough to visit him. In the good weather he plays outside. He builds ramps and tunnels for his Matchbox cars in a huge sand pile behind his house. Or he plays with Cuddles, his one-hundred-pound dog. Jeff throws sticks and tennis balls across the lawn and Cuddles races after them. Jeff has to be careful not to get Cuddles too excited. He could easily tip the wheelchair over. If Cuddles were to jump on him, Jeff could be in trouble because his legs are sensitive to pain. Cuddles seems to understand, and he plays gently with Jeff.

In the house, Jeff has a hard time moving his wheelchair around because of the wall-to-wall carpeting. So his parents bought him a scooter. It's plastic, strong but lightweight, and has wheels that turn easily in any direction. Jeff lies on his scooter and pulls or pushes himself around with his hands. He likes to play on the tile floor in the kitchen. His cars and trucks are lined up there waiting for Jeff when he comes home from school.

Jeff can play with Dan and Jamie using his scooter and their Big Wheel bikes. Jeff's mother carries him down to the basement and lays him on the scooter. Then the fun begins. Dan or Jamie ties a rope from his bike to Jeff's scooter. The brothers take turns towing Jeff around the basement in a big circle, faster and faster.

"I don't have to do anything," Jeff says. "They do all the work, and I have all the fun!"

Jeff's mother is afraid of what may happen if his scooter tips over, or if it crashes into the furnace or a wall. Jeff tells her not to worry. She tries to relax because she knows that it's natural for kids to want to play rough games.

Jeff needs help getting in and out of his wheelchair. He can't dress himself completely because his legs are too stiff and painful to bend. He's still little enough to be carried, so one of his parents lifts him into bed, carries him up and down stairs, and helps him in the bathroom.

When he's not on his scooter playing, Jeff likes to sit on the living room sofa. From there he can watch television or read or play with toys and still be a part of whatever the rest of his family is doing.

Jeff's mother drives him to school and back home again at the end of each day. They leave his wheelchair at home because he has the use of another one in school. Some kids with disabilities learn in special classrooms with a teacher trained to work with the disabled. But Jeff, like Lizzy Kaser, is mainstreamed. A teacher's aide helps him with his books and papers. Sometimes she pushes his wheelchair from one place to another. Usually Jeff moves the chair wheels by himself.

Jeff enjoys gym period, but he can't always participate.

Indoor baseball is one sport he can play, either on a floor scooter or from his wheelchair. Because of the practice he gets with his brothers at home, he has learned to hit balls from a sitting up or lying down position. He likes to run the bases in his wheelchair, but sometimes he chooses a pinch runner from his team.

Four days a week after school, Jeff's mother drives him to Syracuse for physical therapy sessions. This is to exercise his arm and leg joints and to stretch his muscles. Jeff doesn't really enjoy these sessions because at the end of the school day he is usually pretty tired. But he understands the importance of these exercise periods, so he doesn't complain too much.

And he gets ice cream on the way home.

For their summer vacation one year, Jeff's family drove to Florida to see Disney World. They left Jeff's wheelchair at home and took his buggy instead. The buggy is made of aluminum and plastic, so it is much lighter than the wheelchair. Also, the buggy folds up, so it can be carried or easily stowed in the car.

But the buggy has no wheels on the sides, so Jeff can't wheel himself as he does in his wheelchair. One of his family pushed Jeff in the buggy as they toured Disney World.

The buggy caused one big problem: it wasn't allowed on the rides, so someone had to miss a ride and guard the buggy. That meant that Jeff's family never got to go on the same rides at the same time. If the buggy were stolen, Jeff's mother or father would have had to carry him. Carrying Jeff from the house to the car is fairly easy, but carrying Jeff all over Disney World would have been hard work. Jeff weighs about seventy pounds.

Except for the rides, Jeff's family discovered that Disney World is one hundred percent wheelchair accessible. This means that people who use wheelchairs can see all the exhibits, eat in the restaurants, and use the bathroom and washing facilities.

One exhibit, however, would have been difficult to see if Jeff had been using his wheelchair. The underwater submarine was a tight squeeze, even in the buggy. But Jeff's family made the effort, and Jeff was able to enjoy the sharks and octopi and make-believe mermaids.

Jeff is part of an active family. They like to go places and do things. Having a family member in a wheelchair makes all this more difficult, but not impossible.

Jeff's mother offers this advice to other families with a child who uses a wheelchair: "Call ahead, be flexible, and bring along a sense of humor."

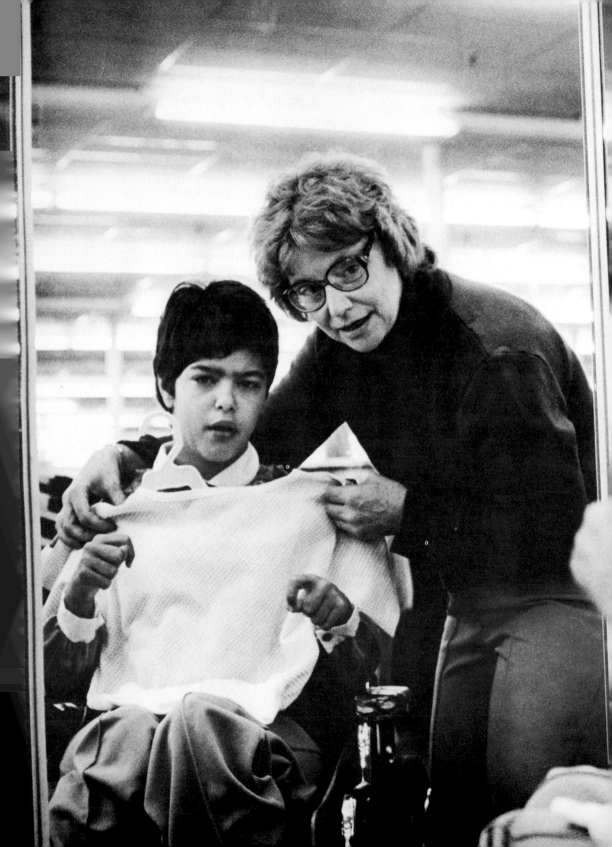

Tammy Knopp

*T*ammy Knopp speaks slowly and carefully. She wants to be understood. "I don't mind talking about me," she says. "I want people to know."

Twelve-year-old Tammy has *cerebral palsy*. Like most other people with this disorder, Tammy does not have full control of her muscles. She uses a wheelchair because she cannot move her leg muscles enough to walk. Her arms and hands are also affected, so she needs someone to push her wheelchair for her. The muscles that control Tammy's speech are impaired so she has difficulty pronouncing some words. Tammy clenches her fingers into fists when she is excited.

At home, Tammy's parents and her three brothers help her. She requires help entering and leaving her house. Someone lifts her into and out of her chair at bedtime. Her mother helps her get dressed and undressed.

At mealtimes, one of her brothers may cut her food, but Tammy likes to feed herself. She uses a spoon holder strapped to her hand, instead of holding the spoon with her fingers. Tammy's mother serves her food in a special plate with raised, curved edges. Tammy can pick up pieces of food without having the food slide off the plate.

Tammy likes to go out to eat in restaurants, but this is not easy. She needs someone to drive her to the restaurant, help her out of the car and into her wheelchair, and wheel her into the building.

Tammy's family has discovered that many restaurants cannot accommodate wheelchairs. One place that Tammy likes has tables too low and too narrow for her wheelchair to slide under. So Tammy sits sideways, making eating even more difficult for her. At the same time, her chair is blocking the aisle, so other customers may bump her as they try to move around her chair.

Tammy is determined, so she still asks to be taken out to eat. She does not like the fact that wheelchair users can't use restaurants as easily as able-bodied people. "Disabled people are part of the world too," she says.

To help Tammy learn how to do things for herself, she attends a special classroom for the disabled in her school. Most of Tammy's school day is spent in this one room. There are three other disabled kids in Tammy's room, plus her teacher and an aide.

Tammy's room is self-contained. This means that she does almost everything right there. Regular subjects are taught in the room, but there are also arrangements for taking naps, eating lunch, and using a bathroom.

But Tammy would rather leave her classroom for some activities. She is taking industrial arts this year, for which she does leave her room.

One corner of the school gymnasium has been reserved for the kids in Tammy's class. They are learning the rules for volleyball. A gym teacher who is trained to work with disabled kids has "borrowed" four able-bodied eighth graders to assist. One of these helpers stands behind each wheelchair. Everyone tries to keep the ball in the air. There is a lot of laughing as the helpers move the wheelchairs and try to position Tammy and her classmates so they can hit the volleyball. Tammy has to have help moving her arms. Her gym teacher holds her wrists, and together they smack the ball when it comes their way. The ball is made of extra light plastic so no one gets hurt.

When Tammy and the others in her room have had enough practice, they will play volleyball in a regular game with able-bodied kids their age. The rules will be changed slightly, and the disabled kids will have helpers playing with them. But Tammy doesn't mind. "Volleyball is exciting," she says.

Like other people who use wheelchairs, Tammy and her family are aware of obstacles. They are alert for buildings that have no ramps or elevators. They avoid public bathrooms unless the doors are wheelchair accessible. Sidewalks with deep ruts and curbs without gentle slopes are especially hard to maneuver in a wheelchair.

Even the weather can make a difference in how a wheelchair user gets around. How do you hold an umbrella while wheeling a wheelchair? Will a wheelchair go through snow? And what happens to it on ice? One day Tammy's wheelchair slid on an icy part of the ramp leading into her school. Her classroom aide lost control of the heavy chair, and it went over the edge onto the hard ground below.

Tammy was strapped into her wheelchair seat, but the seat was not strapped into the chair. Tammy and her seat fell out of the chair when it struck the ground. Tammy had a black eye, a bloody nose and several bruises when she was taken to the nurse's office.

The accident scared Tammy. She still has a real fear of

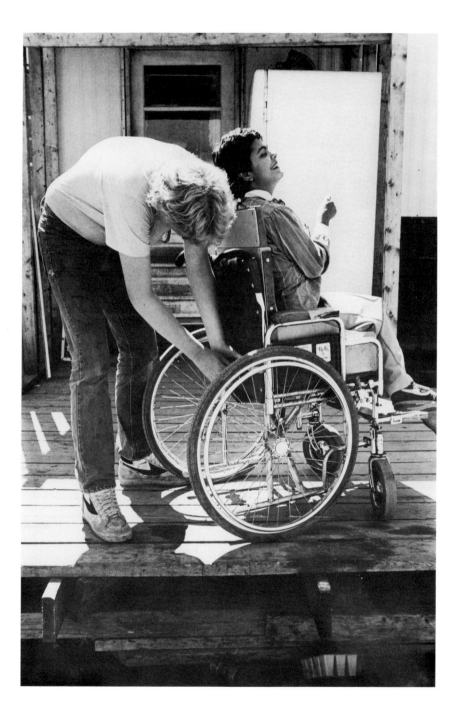

falling. She was angry that someone forgot to strap her special seat into her chair that day. But she realizes that seeing to the securing of her seat is also her responsibility. "Now I remind everyone," she says.

Tammy sees a physical therapist twice each week. The therapist takes Tammy out of her wheelchair and places her on a floor mat. She helps Tammy roll from side to side, from her back to her belly. Together they do several different exercises to relax Tammy's muscles. One that Tammy likes requires that she lie on a huge, soft ball. Her therapist assists her as she rocks slowly back and forth, using some of the muscles that are inactive when she sits in her wheelchair.

At home Tammy likes to play Monopoly with her brothers. She can shake and toss the dice, but one of her brothers helps her move around the board and count out her money. Sometimes Tammy dictates letters while her mother writes down the words.

Tammy finds most television shows boring, except for bowling. She enjoys watching bowling because it is one of the few sports she can participate in. Her family takes her to a bowling alley near their home. Other disabled people bowl there also, some, like Tammy, from a wheelchair.

Because Tammy's hands and fingers can't support the weight of a bowling ball, she uses a special ramp. The ramp is set in front of Tammy, and the ball is placed on top of the ramp. Tammy aims with her eyes, then shoves the ball. It slides down the ramp, and rolls down the alley.

When asked what she likes best about bowling, Tammy smiles and answers, "Strikes!"

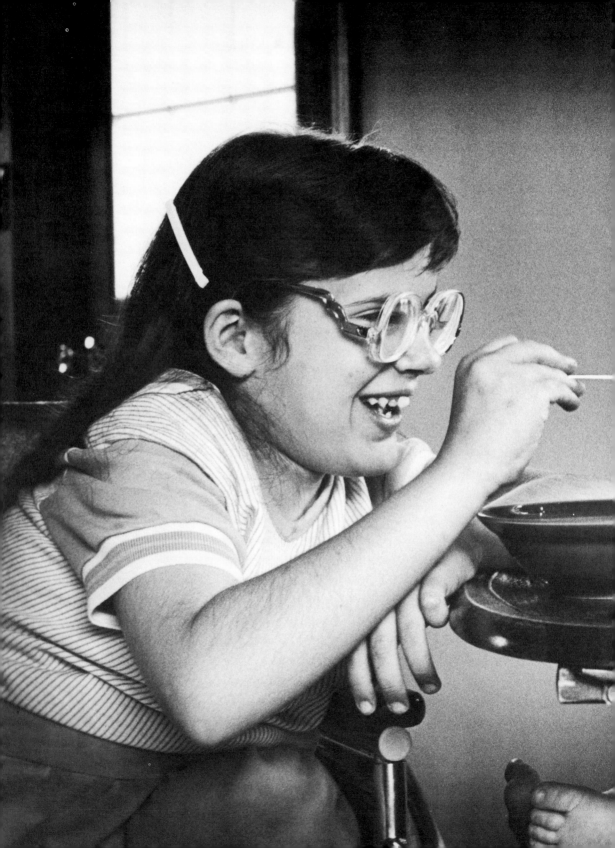

Liz Purtell

*I*f you visit Leighton Elementary School in Oswego, New York, Liz Purtell may pass you in the hall. Hazel eyes and a mischievous smile greet you as Liz wheels herself along in her wheelchair.

When Liz was born, the doctor noticed a small hole in her back, about the size of a half-dollar. Part of Liz's spinal cord protruded through this hole. Because of exposure to the air, the spinal cord and its nerves were damaged. This birth defect is known as *spina bifida*.

Twelve-year-old Liz is partially paralyzed from the waist down, so she uses a wheelchair. She lives with her large family in a comfortable old farmhouse in the country. She moves herself around the house and yard, using the ramp that her father had built near the side door. He lifts her up and down the stairs to her bedroom on the second floor. Recently, Liz's family decided to sell their house. They plan to build a new

one with all the rooms on one level. The house is being designed so that Liz's wheelchair will be accessible to every
room.

Liz is learning to walk on crutches with braces on her legs.
The braces are made of steel, cover the full length of her legs,
and lock and unlock at the knee. "The braces are a pain," Liz
says, "and too heavy."

Sometimes she uses a walker instead of the crutches. The
walker is waist-high, is made of aluminum, and has four legs
to support Liz. It will be a while before she can walk well
enough with any of these aids to do without a wheelchair.

The yard around Liz's house is fairly flat, so she can wheel

her chair there with little difficulty. The muscles in her arms have become strong and well developed from all the extra use they get. She even goes across the road to use a neighbor's swimming pool in the warm weather. Because she cannot kick her legs, Liz has not learned to swim. But she likes to splash in the water, and just float around to cool off. Her friends help her out of her wheelchair and into the pool.

When she goes to the plaza mall with her mother, Liz usually shops by herself. Some people stare at this little girl wandering around alone in a wheelchair. "Just because I'm little, they think I'm too young to be by myself," Liz says. "But I'm almost thirteen."

Some of Liz's girlfriends walk with her into town. They usually let Liz wheel herself, but sometimes they push the chair for her.

Liz's bladder is also paralyzed. She had special surgery, and now her urine bypasses her bladder and goes into a plastic bag worn under her clothes. The bag has to be emptied during the day, so Liz carries paper cups in her book bag. This routine works fine at home and in school. But if Liz visits a friend whose bathroom is upstairs, she needs help emptying the paper cups. One of her friends says Liz is lucky because she never has to worry about finding a bathroom when she needs to void.

Two of Liz's brothers wrestle on the high school team. Liz loves to go to the matches. The other boys on the wrestling team adopted Liz as the team mascot. Liz thought this was great. "I get to sit by the bench near all the guys."

One night the team invited Liz into the center of the gym.

The coach's son presented her with a rose. Then he bent down and kissed her on the cheek, in front of everyone. "It was pretty embarrassing," Liz says. "But it made me happy and I cried." So did her mother and many of the other spectators.

There have been sad times also. Liz had a crush on a boy in her school. He called her often and sent her notes and gifts. One day Liz came home and told her mother that she and the boy had broken up. "He said he still likes me," Liz told her mother. "But he just can't picture marrying me and walking down the aisle with a girl in a wheelchair." Liz can laugh about that incident now, but when it happened, it hurt.

Whenever people ask Liz what's wrong with her, she tells them she was born with spina bifida, and that she's disabled. "I hate the word *crippled*," Liz says. She doesn't mind when people are curious about why she uses a wheelchair. But if any kids tease her she's likely to tell them, "I may be in a wheelchair, but you're a jerk!"

Liz's schedule is pretty much like that of her able-bodied friends. She goes to regular classes in school, comes home to homework, has dinner with her family, and watches television. When girlfriends come to visit, they play with dolls, cards and games and call boys on the telephone.

One of Liz's friends has cerebral palsy and uses a wheelchair. She used to visit Liz often when they were both younger. But now she's much bigger than Liz, and Liz's mother can no longer lift her out of her wheelchair. Now that Liz's new house will have a ramp, her friend can visit more often.

Very few of Liz's school friends live near her, so she spends a lot of time with her brothers and sisters. They play softball, throw sticks and balls for their cocker spaniel Ginger, and go for drives in the family van. Liz's wheelchair locks into a special device in the van to keep it from moving. The family even drove to Disney World in Florida. Because of careful planning, the wheelchair was not a problem for Liz or her family. When they slept in motels, they chose only those that could accommodate the chair. They looked for wide doors and ramps instead of stairs. When they ate in restaurants, they asked first if a wheelchair would fit under a table or at a booth.

Liz is one of the few disabled people in her neighborhood, school and town. Sometimes people stare at her. When this happens Liz gets angry. Her mother has explained that people stare because they are curious; they don't mean to be cruel.

Liz wishes these people would talk to her instead of just looking at her. "Staring isn't nice," Liz says. "I want to be treated nicely."

Scott Laffan

*L*ike Tammy Knopp, Scott Laffan has cerebral palsy. But unlike Tammy, he cannot speak except for a few words. Whereas Tammy sometimes feeds herself after her mother cuts her food up, Scott needs more help. His mother has to feed him because he cannot control the muscles in his hands.

Fourteen-year-old Scott attends a regular middle school, but like Tammy, learns in a special class for disabled kids. Scott is very intelligent, but since he cannot speak, it is often hard to know what's on his mind. In order to help Scott communicate more easily, he is learning to type.

He wears a headband with a long wooden pointer attached to it. Scott's classroom aide puts a piece of paper into the typewriter and sets the margins. Scott bends his head over and strikes the typewriter keys with the tip of the pointer. Typing this way is slow and difficult. But since he may never speak well, typing is one of Scott's ways to communicate.

Scott has another way of making conversation. He uses a Bliss board and points to words or symbols with his head pointer. The board is large and flat. It lays across the arms of Scott's wheelchair. There are over a hundred letters and symbols for Scott to select from when he wants to communicate something. The Bliss board allows him to indicate simple messages faster than if he typed them. For this reason Scott has a Bliss board at school, one at home, and even one at his summer camp.

Scott points to the letter *Y* when he wants to say yellow. His head pointer touches the letter *R* when he wants to tell you that his favorite ballplayer is Reggie Jackson. But spelling takes a lot of time if you are using a head pointer. So, many common words are represented by pictures or symbols on Scott's Bliss board. For example, the symbol ⊢ means toilet. If Scott wants to use the bathroom, he points to that picture on his board and his aide knows what he is trying to tell her.

Scott knows that people sometimes don't understand what he is communicating. He is always happy when he's gotten his message across to another person. He smiles and nods his head vigorously, breathing a soft "yes."

At home Scott's mother does most things for him. She feeds him, dresses him, bathes him, and lifts him into and out of his wheelchair. Scott uses a special toilet seat for extra

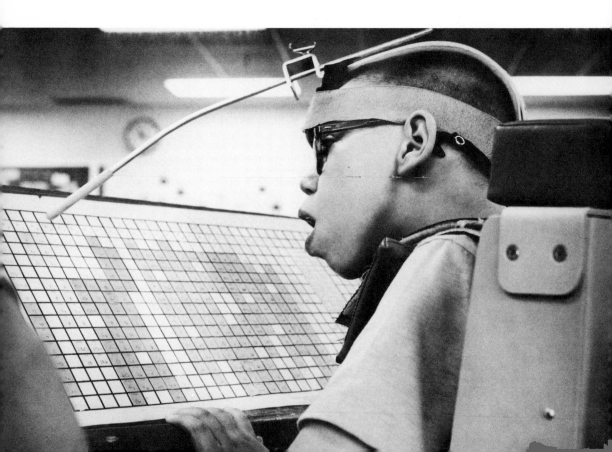

support. In the bathtub, he sits on a small chair. This keeps him upright and makes bathing him easier for his mother.

Scott has a typewriter at home as well as at school. When he has homework, even math, he does it on his typewriter. The typewriter keys are covered with a special plastic sheet so Scott's pointer won't slip when he strikes a key. As at school, someone has to help Scott get set up for doing his work. Once his mother has strapped his headband in place and put his homework sheet in the typewriter, Scott proceeds by himself. He is proud of the things he can do without assistance.

Over the years, Scott and his mother have worked out their own ways of communicating. She has learned to interpret his eye movements, hand signals, mouth motions. When all these fail, Scott points out his needs on the Bliss board.

Still, at times Scott's mother cannot understand right away what Scott is trying to tell her. When this happens Scott becomes annoyed. Eventually, his mother always figures out what he wants, but it sometimes takes a little while. She and Scott have learned to be patient with each other.

Scott has two wheelchairs. He uses a regular, manual wheelchair at home, and his mother pushes it for him. But at school Scott has learned to drive a motorized chair. It is operated by two large batteries strapped to a small platform on the back of the chair. The batteries are connected by wires to a lever on the wheelchair arm. Many wheelchair users call this lever a *joy stick*. Scott has enough hand control to push this stick when he wants to move his chair.

Scott and his mother live in an apartment, on the first

floor. There is only one step, so Scott's mother can move his chair easily in and out. On pleasant days Scott enjoys sitting out in the small yard in front of his apartment. The neighbors know him and usually stop to visit as they pass by. When he sees a friend approaching, Scott throws his head back and laughs. He rocks back and forth and waves his arms. This is Scott's way of saying "Hi, I'm glad to see you!"

Scott's mother often wheels him to the local shopping plaza. One day a little girl walked up to Scott's wheelchair and stood there, staring at him. When Scott noticed, he lowered his head and hid his face. He didn't like being stared at, but he could not tell this to the girl. Scott told his mother later, "I want to be treated like a person, not stared at because I'm disabled." But he had to type the message.

Scott has an active sense of humor. He likes to tease. One of his little tricks is to pretend he doesn't understand what is being said to him. You might ask him a simple question. He will look at you blankly, so you will try to ask it in an easier way. Then slowly he starts to grin when he sees that he's fooled you. His mother says that because he is so often misunderstood, he likes to see how other people react when Scott pretends not to understand *them*.

Because Scott needs help with so many things, some people think he can do nothing at all for himself. But in the yard one day he reached over and raised a neighbor's shirt cuff for a peek at the man's watch. The neighbor looked amazed that Scott could tell the time. Scott and his mother laughed. They both knew Scott wanted to go inside to watch a Yankees' game on television.

Scott enjoys school, because he likes to learn as many new things as he can. But like most kids, his favorite time of year is summer. Then he has more time for sitting outside and visiting with friends. And counting the days till he goes to camp.

Scott attends Camp Goodwill, which is designed for disabled kids. Scott's uncle drives him there for two weeks in July every summer. The camp buildings have ramps for easy accessibility. The doors are wider than usual. The toilet stalls are big enough to admit a wheelchair, and have handles on the walls so the kids can hold on while getting out of their wheelchairs.

The counselors at Camp Goodwill are trained to work with disabled children. Like Scott, many of the kids cannot participate fully in all the activities. But the counselors make sure each camper enjoys some of his favorite things. Scott enjoys floating in the pool and camping out.

For these two weeks in the summer, Scott and his mother have some time away from each other. Scott enjoys being around his camp friends. His mother enjoys having more time to herself. At the end of Scott's camp stay, they are glad to see each other again.

Twice a week, Scott visits the school physical therapist. The therapist exercises Scott's arms and legs and back. These exercises help strengthen his muscles and prevent them from becoming stiff from not being used.

Scott's physical therapist, like his teachers and his mother, helps him in important ways. But as Scott grows older, he will develop some of the skills for taking care of himself. Like many disabled adults, he may live in an apartment or home especially equipped for him. He may live alone, or with another person. He may live in a building with an elevator. If he lives on the ground floor, the building will have a ramp. He may get weekly visits from a physical therapist. A community helper may bring him groceries or take him shopping.

What kind of job will Scott look for? Will he go to college? Scott's mother says that Scott has not begun to think about these questions. He likes school and the Yankees. He enjoys people. For now, for Scott, this seems to be enough.

Mark Manipole

When fifteen-year-old Mark Manipole was only two, his parents noticed that his leg muscles seemed extra large. Later, when he was in kindergarten, his teacher nicknamed him Moose because he was so sturdy for his age. Then the gym teacher saw that Mark was having trouble walking on the balance beam.

Mark's parents had Mark checked by their doctor. He diagnosed *muscular dystrophy*, a disease that weakens the muscles. From that time on, Mark's muscles grew weaker, until he needed a wheelchair for getting around.

Mark still uses a wheelchair. It is battery powered because he does not have full use of his hands. His chair moves only when Mark activates it with the lever attached to the chair arm. Mark has almost complete mobility with his motorized wheelchair. He can travel in and out of his house, down the street to visit friends, to the village mall to shop or play video games.

Mark attends a regular school and is mainstreamed into regular classes. But for gym class he does something special: he leaves the school building and enters a bus that has been converted into a mobile gymnasium for disabled kids.

From the outside it looks like an ordinary yellow school bus. But the seats have been taken out and replaced by mats, balls, an exercise bike, lacrosse sticks, a rowing machine, a small trampoline, a low balance beam and an assortment of other gym equipment. "I can do almost anything in the bus that other kids do in the regular gym," Mark says.

Besides athletic equipment, the bus offers the use of pegboard activities, games, even a "busy box" with buttons, zippers and snaps designed to improve hand and eye coordination.

A special door has been cut into the side of the bus, near the rear. Mark's gym teacher opens the door and lowers a hydraulic elevator. Mark maneuvers his wheelchair onto the elevator platform. His teacher pushes a button and Mark slowly rises until he can move right into the bus.

Each week Mark's gym teacher drives the 1967 school bus-gym to six different schools. He works with one disabled kid at a time, in order to give each the attention he or she needs.

One of Mark's favorite activities in the mobile gym is catching a ball with a lacrosse stick. His gym teacher lifts him out of his wheelchair and sits him on a floor mat with a wall for back support. Mark warms up with a few arm and leg stretches, helped by his teacher. Then he smacks at a tetherball suspended from the ceiling. When Mark's gym teacher feels Mark's muscles are limber enough, he brings out the lacrosse stick.

The stick hangs from the ceiling in front of Mark, chin high. Mark's teacher helps him grasp the stick with both hands. The stick supports Mark's arms, and he moves it back and forth and from side to side. His gym teacher kneels about fifteen feet in front of Mark with his own lacrosse stick. They play catch until Mark tires.

Before Mark returns to the school building, he often manipulates pegs into a board to improve the muscle coordination in his hands and fingers. His gym teacher times him to see if there is improvement from week to week.

At home in his bedroom, Mark exercises his arm muscles. A rope passes through a pulley screwed into the ceiling. Mark holds one end of the rope in each hand. He yanks one hand down, pulling the weight of the other hand and arm up into the air. He does this every night before he goes to bed. He finds this exercise boring, but he knows it's good for strengthening his arms.

Other than visiting a mobile gym and a private gym teacher, the rest of Mark's school day is the same as that of his able-bodied friends. After school he is driven home in a van with six other kids who use wheelchairs. The chairs wheel up a ramp, and are locked into place once inside the van.

Because Mark's wheelchair is motorized, he can maneuver his sloping driveway and the ramp his father built onto their

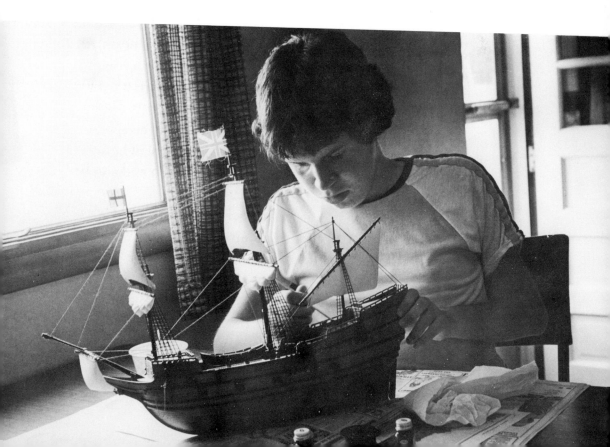

front porch. There are no steps in his house, so Mark can move easily from room to room. The television set, refrigerator and stereo equipment are all accessible to him in his sitting position.

Mark's parents have made their house and yard wheelchair accessible for Mark. They help him in and out of the chair, but if he drops something he picks it up himself. He uses a long stick with a "grabber" on one end, because he cannot bend over far enough to pick up dropped items with his hands.

When Mark leaves his neighborhood, however, he finds that not all situations are as easily controlled. Mark couldn't see a dentist for a long time because his mother was unable to find one whose office was either on the first floor or accessible by elevator.

The building where Mark's pediatrician has his office used to be equipped with a wheelchair ramp. Then the landlord had the ramp removed. Now Mark can see his doctor only if his father carries him into the building. This is embarrassing for Mark and unpleasant for his father. Mark weighs over a hundred pounds and is tall for his age.

Mark's church has made an effort to meet his needs by installing an elevator. Now Mark can attend church whenever he wants to. The elevator is operated with a key, and can be used by anyone unable to climb stairs.

Except for buildings without ramps or elevators, Mark is mostly independent unless something goes wrong with his wheelchair. That sometimes happens. As Mark was coming home from the mall one day, his chair struck a bump. The plug that connects the batteries to the control box came out of the socket. From his seat, Mark cannot reach the plug or the socket. So he sat and waited. About a half hour later, a neighbor drove by and happened to notice Mark stranded. He reinserted the plug and Mark motored home.

It is Mark's responsibility to make sure his batteries get recharged every night before he goes to bed. He asks his father or mother to plug the batteries into a charger kept in his room. In the morning the batteries are ready to be used again. "If I forget to remind someone, I'm grounded," Mark says. "So I don't forget."

Mark likes to be active, even though he can't do everything he'd like to do. His friend Maureen took him water-skiing in Canada one summer. He wore a life jacket and sat on a special board shaped like a short surfboard. Mark held the rope while Maureen sat behind and held Mark around the waist. Was he scared? "Terrified the first time," Mark says. How did it feel to water-ski sitting while other skiers stood up? Mark smiles. "Why stand up when you can sit down?" he says.

A quieter sport for Mark is giving his four-year-old neighbor rides on his wheelchair. Using his hands, Mark lifts his feet off their metal rest plate. There is just enough room for his friend to sit. They ride up and down the driveway with Mark at the controls and his friend yelling for him to go faster.

Most of Mark's friends are his age. Some are older, with drivers' licenses. Mark is already making plans to learn to drive the family van when he turns sixteen. The van would

have to be customized with hand controls instead of foot pedals.

In the meantime, one of Mark's friends, who is disabled with muscular dystrophy, has offered to teach Mark to drive his own specially equipped van. The plan is to have Mark drive in an empty parking lot where no one could get hurt. Mark understands that driving an automobile is more tricky than driving his wheelchair. But he's ready to give it a try.

Mark's advice to other disabled kids is to "have a good sense of humor. It's best not to feel sorry for yourself. Just do whatever you can, and to heck with the rest."

Even Mark's sense of humor doesn't let him laugh off some things. One day a little boy came up to Mark in a pizza shop. Before they could strike up a conversation, the boy's mother grabbed his hand and hurried him away. This made Mark angry.

A happier moment came when Mark was invited by the Syracuse University lacrosse team to see one of their games. They sent him a program in which all the players had signed their names beneath their pictures, with little notes to Mark. They also sent two free tickets, so Mark invited his father to accompany him to the game.

During a break in the game the team captain came and sat with Mark in the bleachers. "About a million people turned to look at me," Mark said. "I felt pretty embarrassed but it was worth it."

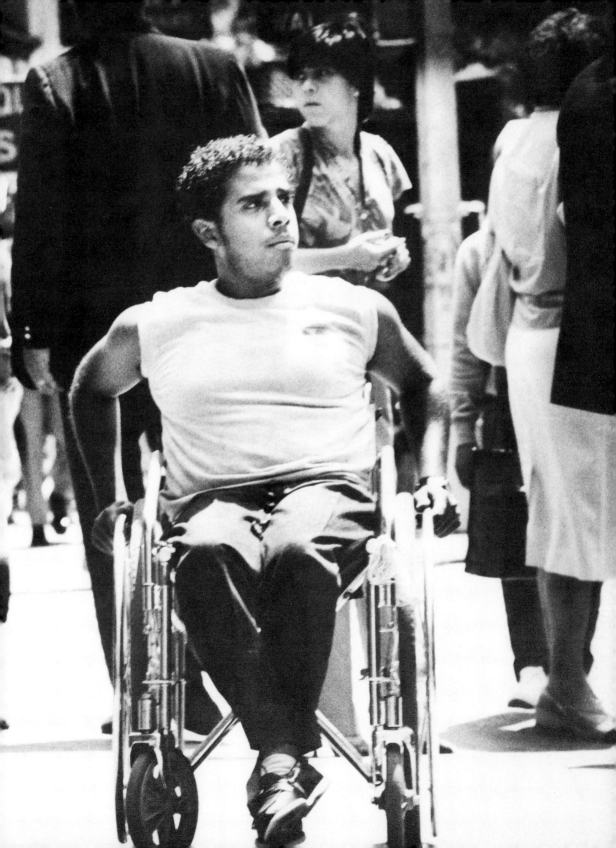

José Rivera

When José Rivera wants to move around New York City where he lives, he has four choices: riding in a taxi, taking a subway, using a city bus, or wheeling his wheelchair. Most often, José gets where he needs to go by himself, in his chair. Taxis are expensive, not all buses can accommodate a person in a wheelchair, and subways are located down a flight of stairs, inaccessible to most wheelchair users.

José was born in Puerto Rico nineteen years ago. He is partially paralyzed from the waist down because he has spina bifida.

When he was five years old, José began using a wheelchair. It was a small chair, built especially for small children. At about age seven, José began walking with crutches or a walker. But as he got older, he grew taller and gained weight. His legs were no longer strong enough to carry him. Now José uses a wheelchair all the time.

The problem José faces in manually wheeling himself around is that Manhattan is very big. It is about twelve miles from one tip of the island to the other. There are hundreds of streets and avenues, millions of people and automobiles. The sidewalks are usually crowded, making wheelchair travel extremely difficult.

José is forced to use buses and taxis now and then, even though he would rather not. His wheelchair is collapsible, and can be stowed next to him on a taxi seat or in the car trunk. If he decides to take a bus, José must wait for one designed to take wheelchairs aboard. Not all New York City buses are so equipped. Those that are have hydraulic plat-

AT THE BROADWAY THEATRE
Cast album on RCA records and cassettes

forms that can be lowered by the driver. When the platform reaches the curb, the wheelchair user rolls his chair onto it and then the platform is raised into the bus.

Once inside the bus, the driver helps the wheelchair user lock his chair so it won't move when the bus does. Most buses that are wheelchair accessible have special areas of the bus, usually near the rear, where chairs can be safely positioned.

More than once José has watched buses pass him by as he waited at a bus stop. "It's discrimination," José says. "The buses are crowded, so the driver keeps going. If he stops, it takes almost five minutes to get my chair inside and locked. I understand, but I don't like it."

José lives with his mother and sister part of the time. At other times, he stays with an older brother or an aunt. But José would rather have his own place. Because even very small, simple apartments in New York are expensive to rent, it may be a while before José can afford to move into his own. For now he will continue to live with his family even though it means less privacy for everyone.

With millions of people seeking jobs in José's city, the competition for employment is stiff. This is especially so for some disabled people. While it might seem unfair and could be illegal, some employers will not hire a person if he cannot walk or use his hands.

Until recently José worked in a hospital as a dispatcher. His job was to make sure that hospital patients who had appointments for treatment or tests in other parts of the hospital got there safely and on time. From his office, José used a

walkie-talkie to direct the men and women who worked for him. These workers would receive a call from José to go to the patient's room and escort the patient to his or her appointment. Then, after the visit was finished, the patient would be escorted back to his room.

José enjoyed his job. It was something he could do well without the use of his legs. Since he is fluent in both Spanish and English, he was a valuable worker. But the hospital made some staff changes in order to save money, and José was laid off.

Now José is looking for another job that he can do in his wheelchair. He has found that getting to job interviews is difficult. Sometimes he leaves two hours early in order to travel one mile in the city. This same distance might take an able-bodied person twenty minutes. But José needs money so he continues to read the want ads and get himself to interviews.

When he is not job hunting, José enjoys doing active things with his friends. Basketball is one sport José can play from his wheelchair. He and a few friends who are also wheelchair users play whenever they have the time.

The rules for wheelchair basketball are similar to those for regular basketball. Some of the skills required are the same, too: fast reflexes, good hand and eye coordination, strong arms. But instead of running around the court, the players wheel their chairs. Sometimes chairs collide. Now and then a chair tips over or a player falls out onto the court. When that happens the game stops until the player is back in his chair, able to continue.

With as many as ten wheelchairs racing around a basketball court, a few hands and fingers are bound to get pinched in between wheels. José has had his share of spills and bruised fingers. "But I still love the sport," José says. "It's exciting to make points from a wheelchair."

When one of José's friends can borrow a car, they like to go camping outside of the city. José spends so much time indoors that he enjoys this change of scenery. He is able to set up his own tent from his wheelchair. He also gathers firewood and does his share of the cooking and pot washing.

If the campsite is near water, José goes in swimming. His arms are powerful from pushing his wheelchair for fifteen

years. He swims well, even though most of his swimming ability is in the upper part of his body.

José stays in good physical condition. He relies on his body, particularly his arms, to get him around the city. Every morning before getting into his wheelchair he does sit-ups and push-ups.

In spite of his ability to maneuver himself around the city, José feels that owning his own car would make travel faster, easier and safer. He would be able to make trips out of New York City more often. Finding a job and an apartment would be easier, José feels, if he could travel by car.

José owned a car when he was sixteen. He saved up $1,400 and bought a 1976 Monte Carlo. His legs weren't strong enough to operate the floor pedals, so José did some customizing. He bought two drain plungers from a hardware store and cut off the rubber suction cups. Using metal clamps, he then attached the wooden poles to the gas and brake pedals. The other ends of the plungers stuck up between his legs as he sat at the steering wheel.

When he wanted gas, José pushed that pole down. If he needed to apply the brake, he shoved the other handle down. That is not the easiest way to drive, but as José says, "it beats walking."

José's brother borrowed his car one day. He hit a deep pothole in the street, and the car went out of control. His brother wasn't hurt, but the Monte Carlo was totalled. It will take José a long time to save money for another car. He receives a monthly disability check from the government, but he gives most of this money to his mother, to help pay the rent and buy food.

At age nineteen José thinks a lot about his future. He hasn't made any definite plans about college or starting a family of his own, but does feel that someday he'd like to do both.

As a disabled young adult, José is looking at all of his options. Some may be more possible for him than others. "I live for today," he says. "I can't control what comes next. I'm healthy; I have my friends. I'll make it."

A Few More Facts

Lizzy Kaser's birth defect is known as *arthrogryposis*. Children born with this condition have stiff joints and weak muscles. The disease begins while the baby is still inside the mother's body, but the cause of the disease is unknown. Children born with arthrogryposis often resemble wooden marionettes, because their arms and legs are stiff. Their limbs are small in circumference. Lizzy, like most children born with this disease, has normal speech and intelligence.

Jeff VanDusen was born with *hemolymphangioma*. He had tumors or lumps over much of his body at birth. These tumors were caused by overgrowth of blood vessels and lymphatic tissue. Sometimes these tumors can be removed surgically. Jeff had some removed, but others were located in parts of his body where doctors felt it was too dangerous to operate.

Tammy Knopp and Scott Laffan have *cerebral palsy*. This is a group of disabling conditions resulting from damage to the central nervous system. Cerebral palsy can be severe, so that a person affected cannot control body movement. Or it can be mild, resulting in perhaps a slight speech impairment. Cerebral palsy is not contagious, usually not hereditary, and not a primary cause of death. But it is one of America's major disablers. About 700,000 Americans have some degree of cerebral palsy, one-third of whom are under age twenty-one. Nearly 10,000 babies are born each year with central nervous system disorders that result in cerebral palsy. Scott and Tammy were two such babies.

Liz Purtell and José Rivera were born with *spina bifida*. This disease was first recognized over 4,000 years ago. At birth, babies with this condition have an opening in their back, usually near the bottom of the spine. Often a section of the spinal cord and its nerves protrude through this hole. The spinal cord can become infected or damaged. This damage usually results in some weakening of the lower body muscles or partial paralysis. One or two babies out of every 1,000 are born with spina bifida.

Mark Manipole's *muscular dystrophy* was noticed when he was five years old. Muscular dystrophy is a group of similar diseases marked by weakness of the skeletal muscles (those which control body movement). This condition is progressive, meaning that the symptoms gradually get worse as muscles deteriorate. So far there is no cure and no way to stop the disease process. Muscular dystrophy is not contagious. It is usually inherited, passed from one generation to the next. Many thousands of Americans suffer from this disease. It can strike anyone, at any age. Almost two-thirds of those affected by muscular dystrophy are children.

Further Reading

Now that you have met Elizabeth, Jeff, Tammy, Liz, Scott, Mark, and José, you may want to read about other disabled kids. Here are some interesting books to look for in your school or public library.

NOVELS

Hermes, Patricia. *What If They Knew?* Harcourt Brace Jovanovich, 1980.

Kent, Deborah. *Belonging.* Dial, 1978.

Kingman, Lee. *Head Over Wheels.* Houghton Mifflin, 1978.

Slepian, Jan. *The Alfred Summer.* Macmillan, 1980. The sequel is *Lester's Turn.* Macmillan, 1981.

NONFICTION

Allen, Anne. *Sports for the Handicapped.* Walker, 1981.

Rosenberg, Maxine B. *My Friend Leslie: The Story of a*

Handicapped Child. Photographs by George Ancona. Lothrop, 1983.

Savitz, Harriet M. *Wheelchair Champions: A History of Wheelchair Sports.* Harper & Row, 1979.

Wolf, Bernard. *Don't Feel Sorry for Paul.* Photographs by the author. Harper & Row, 1974.

Index

communication
  by Bliss board, 45-46
  hand, eye, mouth
    movements with
    mother, 47
  using typewriter, 44, 47
  enjoyment of outdoors, 48,
    49-51
  maternal care highly
    necessary, 44,
    46-47, 48
  school, special class in, 44
  self-care, hope for, 51
  sense of humor, 48
  separate wheelchairs
    for home and for
    school, 47

Mainstreaming of
  handicapped students,
  11, 20, 38, 55
Manipole, Mark, 52-61
  exercise at home for
    muscle improve-
    ment, 57
  motorized wheelchair,
    complete mobility
    with, 54, 57-58
  battery recharging, his

responsibility for, 59
muscular dystrophy
  victim, 54, 74
planning to drive family
  van when sixteen,
  59-61
need for hand controls,
  59-61
riding young kids on
  chair's footrest, 59
school
  gym classes special,
    55-56
  mainstreamed into
    regular classes, 55, 57
  sense of humor, need
    for, 61
  water skiing, 59
Muscular dystrophy, 54,
  74-75

Public Law 94-142, 2
Purtell, Liz, 32-41
  activities
    play with siblings, 40
    shopping, 37
    "swimming," 37
    watching wrestling,
      37-38